The Lost City

Written and Illustrated
by
Captain Chuck Harman

In an uncharted region of the steamy South American rain forest, Eduardo the Explorer searched for answers to ancient mysteries. Working for days and finding nothing did not deter Eduardo. He kept on digging, looking for clues. One day, his shovel struck something hard. He uncovered an old clay pot with a scroll of paper in it. Careful not to tear the tattered parchment, he slowly removed it from the pot. "Oh, my gosh!" whispered Eduardo under his breath. "It's a map!"

Quickly, Eduardo slipped the map into a pouch and tucked it safely away inside his fuselage. He made his way through the jungle to a clearing. He looked around, checked out the height of the trees and the direction of the wind. Satisfied that he could make it safely, Eduardo began his takeoff roll.

In the air, Eduardo's mind began to race. His heart was pounding and his wingtips were sweaty. "What should I do with the map?" he thought to himself. "Who should I show it to? What if it's a treasure map? This could be dangerous." Eduardo decided that the only plane who could help him was his old friend, Artie the Airplane.

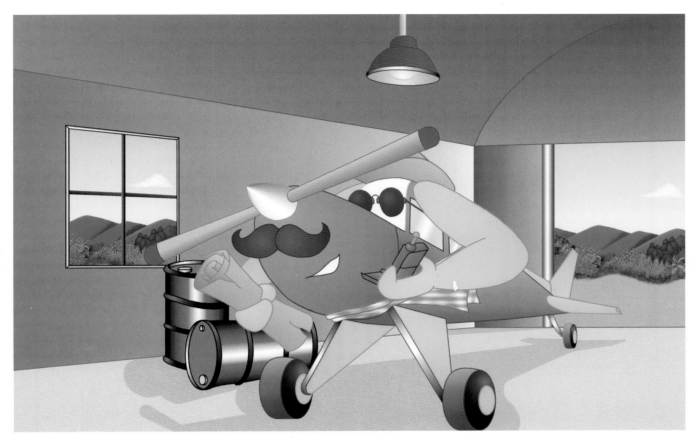

When Eduardo landed, he rushed to the phone and dialed Artie's number. Eduardo examined the map and began planning the search as he waited for Artie to answer. "We'll travel deep into the rain forest following the map," he thought to himself. "The only other people we will tell is Gramma and Grampa Cubbie. Someone has to know where we are and what we're doing."

The rescue phone woke Artie from his sleep. He fumbled for the phone in the dark. "Hello?" answered Artie.

"Artie, you have to come down here right away. I've found a map!" explained an excited Eduardo.

"A map?" questioned Artie. "What kind of map?" he asked, still very groggy.

"I think it's a treasure map," whispered Eduardo into the phone.

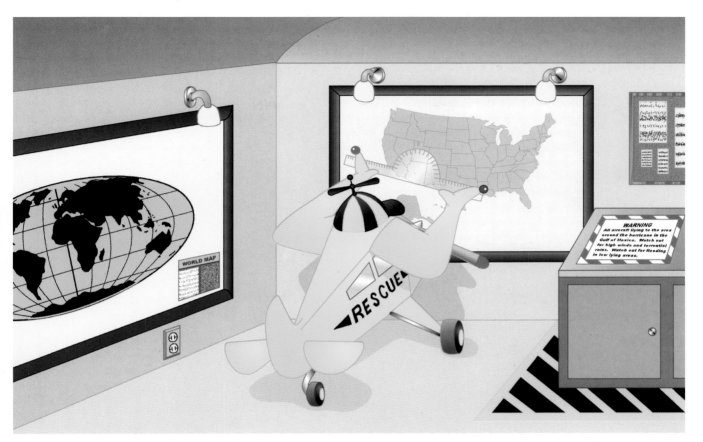

Suddenly, Artie was wide-awake. He asked Eduardo what supplies he needed to bring with him. Eduardo and Artie discussed the details. After gathering up everything he would need, planning the route and checking the weather, Artie took-off for South America.

The flight took Artie across Mexico and Central America. After what seemed like endless hours of flying, Artie landed in Ecuador and met up with Eduardo.

Artie and Eduardo took off together and began the perilous journey through the high passes of the Andes. Once they made it through the mountains, they flew over the rain forest to the clearing in the jungle, near where Eduardo had found the map.

After landing, Artie and Eduardo started hiking through the jungle. Artie had never been in the jungle before. Everything about the jungle was new and unknown to him. Feeling a little bit unsure, Artie asked Eduardo, "Do we have to hike through the jungle? I'd feel safer if we flew."

Eduardo reassured his friend that everything was okay. "It's just a bit further Artie. Come on."

Finally, Eduardo reached into his pouch and pulled out the map. He said, "Okay Artie, we're here. Let's figure out where to go and what to look for." The two planes studied the pictures on the map. They each had very different ideas on what the symbols meant, but both of them agreed that they were directions to a lost city. Eduardo and Artie decided to fly a search pattern in the sky looking for ancient ruins.

As they flew, Artie and Eduardo investigated many things in the jungle that looked promising, but, time after time, they turned out to be nothing. Artie was getting tired, and a little disappointed that they had not found anything after so much searching. Artie said, "I don't see anything but jungle down there, Eduardo. Are you sure we're looking in the right place?"

Eduardo saw a clearing in the jungle. "There's a place to land below us, let's stop and look at the map again," he said. Eduardo flew low over the clearing to make sure it was safe to use as a runway. Then, both of the planes landed and taxied to a shady spot to look at the map.

"I think the arrow means we should fly south from where you found the map," said Artie.

Eduardo didn't agree. "I don't think it means fly south, I think it means follow the river," said Eduardo.

"Which river, Eduardo?" asked Artie. "There must be hundreds of rivers in the rain forest."

Suddenly, the ground beneath them gave way. Artie and Eduardo fell through the opening into an enormous cave. "Aaaaaaaahhhhhhhhh," they yelled out as they fell. After a minute of complete panic, Eduardo looked at Artie and said, "Um, Artie? What are we doing? We're airplanes. We don't fall-we fly." Slightly embarrassed, Artie and Eduardo rolled over, and started to laugh. They couldn't believe that they had forgotten they could fly.

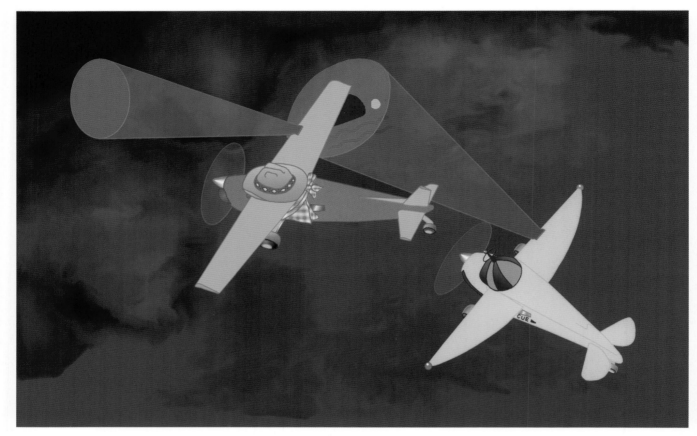

The two planes began to explore the huge cave. The cave was enormous and they were not sure how to get out. As they flew, the cave began to get darker and darker. Eduardo turned on his lights, so he could see where he was going. As he flew, his lights passed over something on the cave wall. "Eduardo! Turn around!" yelled Artie. "I saw something!" Eduardo quickly rolled into a steep-banked turn.

Artie and Eduardo lined up, side-by-side, to get as much light on the wall as possible. Through the darkness, a picture began to appear. "It's the second picture on the map!" the boys cried out together.

Eduardo exclaimed, "The red arrow must have meant down. Down into the cave!"

Artie said, "You're right Eduardo. So what does this one mean?"

Eduardo answered, "I don't know, Artie, let's keep looking!"

The two explorers flew on. "I'm starting to get a little worried, Eduardo," said Artie. "I'm running low on fuel. We need to find a way out of here soon." Eduardo reassured Artie that they would find their way out if they used their heads. "I know," said Artie. "I'll call Shirley the Skyvan on my radio. She knows all about this kind of flying!"

"Skyvan 86 Sierra Victor this is Artie, over."
The radio crackled back, "This is 86 Sierra Victor, Hi Artie, it's Shirley, what's up?" Artie explained the predicament he and Eduardo were in and asked for help. Shirley told Artie to listen for the sound of running water, find it and follow it out of the cave. "Thank you, Shirley," said Artie. "I just knew you'd be able to help."

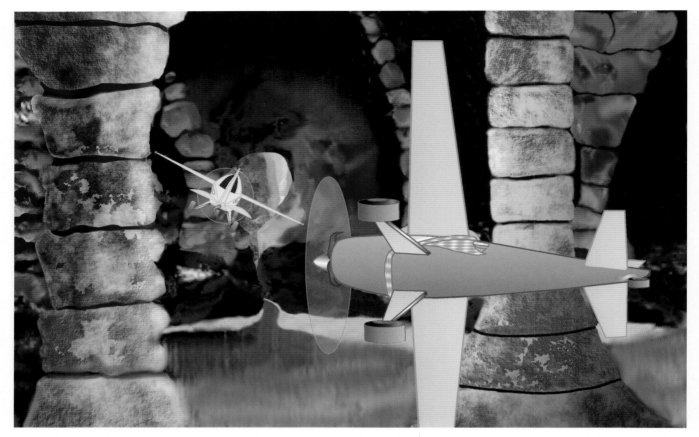

The boys found a river and began to follow it. They saw more writing on the walls, and more signs of civilization. The cave was getting lighter, so Artie and Eduardo turned off their lights. The two planes entered a giant section of cave, with tall columns of rock everywhere. Eduardo spotted an opening in the cave wall. "Look, Artie!" exclaimed an excited Eduardo. "There's the way out!"

Artie and Eduardo flew out of the cave and found themselves in a beautiful, jungle valley. "Artie, look!" exclaimed Eduardo. "I know," said Artie. "There's the palm trees, and the waterfall, just like on the map." The two planes strained to climb over the falls. "Keep going, Artie," said Eduardo. "We have to make it over. There's not enough room to turn around." The boys struggled, but never gave up, and finally made it over the top.

In the distance, there was a giant beacon of light. "Artie! This way," shouted Eduardo. As the two planes flew towards the light, they began to see evidence of ancient ruins in the jungle below. Artie and Eduardo were very excited. They knew they were on the right track and soon they would find the lost city.

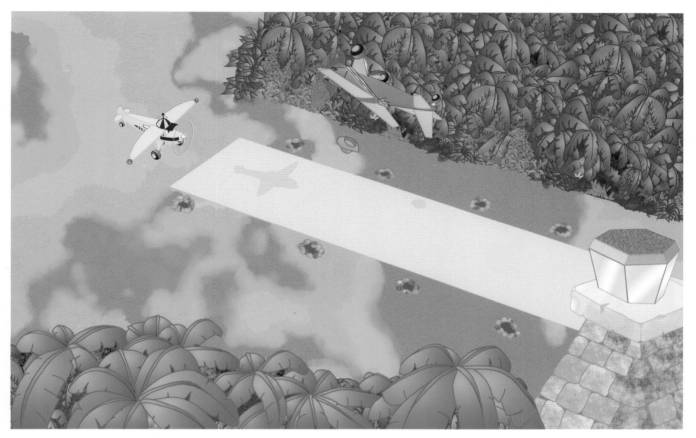

"Eduardo, look!" shouted Artie. He didn't need to tell Eduardo. Eduardo saw it too. It was an old control tower on top of a pyramid of carefully cut stones. Below the tower, on the floor of the jungle, lay an ancient airport. "Yahoo!" shouted out Eduardo. "Yippee!" exclaimed Artie. The two planes pulled up into a steep climb and began their approach to the runway. Eduardo even rolled over and his hat fell off, onto one of the taxiways. The two friends were giddy with excitement as they landed.

Once on the ground, Artie and Eduardo began to look around. "Eduardo?" asked Artie. "This airport is not very run down for a place that's supposed to be lost." Eduardo looked around. "You're right, Artie," said Eduardo. Suddenly, the boys felt a little uneasy. They felt as if something or someone was watching them from the jungle. "I don't think we should be here," said Artie, as he began to taxi back towards the runway. Eduardo said, "Wait for me!"

All at once, many fierce-looking planes appeared from the jungle. The planes began to circle around Artie and Eduardo, until they were completely surrounded. Just when Artie and Eduardo thought that they were in the biggest trouble of their entire lives, one of the planes spoke up; "Soy el Jefe de Los Aeroplanos de la Selva Tropical. Bienvenidos amigos."

Eduardo let out a big sigh of relief. Artie didn't understand what the plane had said, but managed a smile. "What did he say, Eduardo?" asked Artie. "He said he is the Chief of the Airplanes of the Rain Forest and that we are welcome here," answered Eduardo.

"How did you find us?" one of the planes asked.

"Where did you come from?" asked another.

The planes gathered around closely to listen to Artie and Eduardo speak. Eduardo showed them the ancient map that he had found and told them of their journey. The Chief explained that they had lived in the same place for hundreds of years and that the map must have been left there long ago. The planes of the rain forest had many questions about the outside world. Artie and Eduardo did their best to answer them all.

Soon, it was Artie and Eduardo's turn to ask some questions. "How many planes live here?" asked Artie.
"Could you show us around?" asked Eduardo.
The Chief told Artie and Eduardo to follow him up the big stone steps to the control tower.

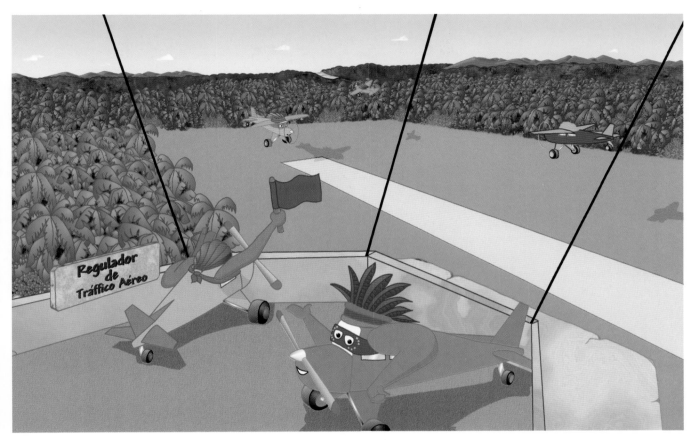

By now many of the planes had taken off and were practicing their landings. "We use colored flags to control the traffic on the runway," said the Chief. "Red means don't land and green means okay to land," he explained.

"Do you see the giant navigation towers everywhere?" he asked. Artie and Eduardo shook their heads yes. "We use the sunlight and the mirrors on top of the towers to help everyone find their way around the jungle," explained the Chief.

Then, The Chief took them into the jungle. "We collect our oil from these pools and bring it to the city in that big pipe made out of stone," he explained.

"This place is amazing," said Artie. Eduardo nodded his head in agreement.

Finally, the Chief took them to the great rock pond, where the planes liked to go to beat the heat of the jungle. "That looks like fun," said Artie to Eduardo, but when he turned around, he saw Eduardo had already climbed up the rocks and was diving into the pool.

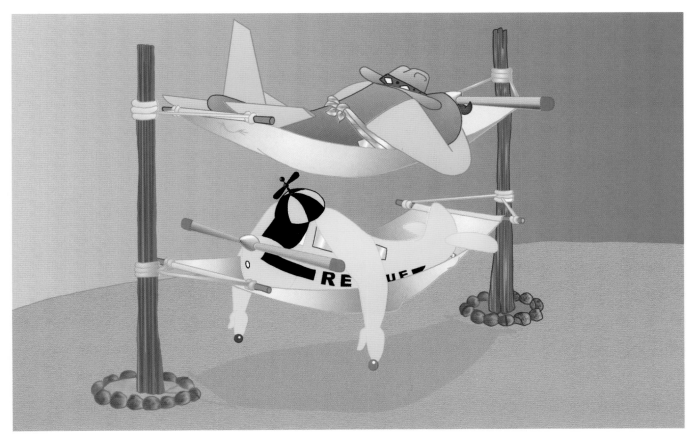

Before going to bed, the two explorers talked about their discovery and their new friends. "These planes are just like us," said Artie. "They just do things differently."

Eduardo agreed, "I guess it doesn't matter where you're from, planes are planes." The boys decided that they would never tell anyone but Gramma and Grampa Cubbie about what they had found. That night, as they slept, their heads were filled with dreams of great adventure.

In the morning, Artie and Eduardo told everyone that they had to return home. They taxied out to the runway with their new friends. Eduardo told the Chief, "We have decided not to let anyone know about this place, but we will leave you a map. It is up to you to decide if you want anyone to know you live here."

Artie and Eduardo took off on their journey home. The Chief flew with them to the great waterfall and showed Artie and Eduardo a pass through the mountains. Then, he bid them a safe journey and returned to his home.

"We are truly awesome explorers," shouted Artie. "We are swashbuckling adventurers!" laughed Eduardo. The two friends flew on, making bolder and bolder claims. They felt a great sense of accomplishment for what they had done.

Artie and Eduardo landed and checked in with Gramma and Grampa Cubbie. They told them the whole story. "We wish we would have found some treasure," said Artie and Eduardo. Grampa Cubbie put his wings around both of them. "You did, boys," he said. "You found some new friends. There is no greater treasure."

Meet a few of

Alice the Air Ambulance

Albert T. Agplane

Becky the Big Tire Blimp

Bubba the Bush Plane

Carlos the Cargo Plane

Codi the Copter

Eduardo the Explorer

Frankie the Fighter

Gilda the Glider

Gramma Cubbie

Grampa Cubbie

Heidi the High Wing

Jack the Jumbo

Jessie the Jet Fuel Truck

Leslie the Low Wing

Artie's friends.

Pete the Patrol Car

Pierre the Plane

Piper

Robert the Rescue Plane

Lt. Sam Sweptwing

San Antonio Sal

Simon the Starfighter

Shirley the Skyvan

Sigmund the Skycrane

Superslim

Tina the Tailwheel

Waldo W. Wing

Wally the Widebody

Bartholomew T. Barnstormer

Captain Chuck

Artiefacts™

What is a windsock?

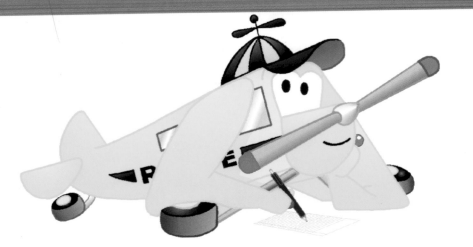

A windsock shows the direction the wind is blowing from. It is also used to estimate the wind speed. Airplanes takeoff and land into the wind. When a windsock stands straight out, the wind is 15 knots, or 17.26 mph.